Danny
The Champion Pony

Suzette Winter

Illustrated with photos from the feature film, "DANNY"

A BANTAM SKYLARK BOOK®
TORONTO • NEW YORK • LONDON • SYDNEY • AUCKLAND

To Rebecca Page
who knows that all it takes is a lot of hard work . . .
and maybe a little love

This low-priced Bantam Book
has been completely reset in a type face
designed for easy reading, and was printed
from new plates. It contains the complete
text of the original hard-cover edition.
NOT ONE WORD HAS BEEN OMITTED.

DANNY
A Bantam Book / published by arrangement with
Random House Inc.

Skylark Books is a registered trademark of Bantam Books, Inc.,
Registered in U.S. Patent and Trademark Office and elsewhere.
Bantam edition / April 1983

ISBN 0-553-15193-2

Published simultaneously in the United States and Canada

PRINTED IN THE UNITED STATES OF AMERICA
C 0 9 8 7 6 5 4

One

The instant Janie Neely saw Danny, she felt her whole life change. He stood at the van ramp in the warm June sunshine, head held high. Then he stared straight down at Janie. His brown eyes were so intelligent. She had waited since early morning for the pony to be delivered. He was just one more animal for the Longvue Farm stable, just one more pony for Andrea Cummings. But to Janie he was special.

The four stable horses gathered at the fence close by. They thrust out their heads, snorting and showing off. They stamped and they whinnied. Danny was not impressed. The new pony was pale gray. His mane and his long tail were white. Bright blue wrappings protected his legs. Pat Chapin held him firmly and stroked his neck to soothe him. She always knew how to calm a horse down. Pat was manager and trainer at Longvue and she knew more about horses and riding than anyone Janie had ever met. Besides, even though she was twenty-four and Janie was only thirteen, Pat was Janie's best friend.

"Hey, wake up down there! Dreaming already?" Pat was laughing. "Meet Danny. Well, what do you think? The question is—will Andrea like him?"

"Oh, yes. Of course she will." Surely anyone would be

delighted to own such a fantastic pony. Janie stepped back
quickly as Danny clattered down the ramp.

"Here. Hold him for a moment while I sign for him." Pat
handed the lead-line to Janie and marched off. The pony
seemed huge. But Janie was not at all afraid. He shook
himself, bending around to look at her.

"Don't be scared, Danny," she said softly. "This is your
new home." He dropped his head and shoved it against
her playfully. He blew gently into her face and nibbled on
a piece of her honey-brown hair. His grassy smell was
sweet. His nose was pink and very soft. Janie patted him.
Then Pat was back, taking the lead-line from her.

4

"Well, you'd better run and tell Andrea her pony's here, Janie."

"You mean she's arrived for the summer? Oh, great!" And Janie was off, racing through the stable yard, up the driveway, leaping flower beds and bounding up steps.

It was quiet in front of the big stone house. The horse van ground its way slowly up a distant hill, and was gone. Janie tried to control her panting, after all that running.

"Andrea . . . Andrea!" She waited, but Andrea's window remained tightly closed. Were they all still asleep? It must be at least ten o'clock. Janie had forgotten her watch again. She pushed open a terrace door.

The paneled room was dim. "Andrea?" Janie stepped carefully across thick carpets.

"Why, Janie, is that really you?"

Janie jumped. Through a distant archway, Mr. Cummings peered at her. Janie saw the long polished dining table and silver coffee service. She tried to smooth her shirt which smelled strongly of horses.

"My goodness, Janie, how you've grown."

Janie smiled uncomfortably. She was still the smallest thirteen-year-old girl in her school. Why did grown-ups always talk about size?

"Mr. Cummings, Andrea's new pony's here." If only she didn't feel so awkward. Just like a little kid. If only Andrea would come downstairs.

"He's here, is he? Andrea will be pleased. Run and tell her. She's probably still in her room." And Mr. Cummings returned to his newspaper.

Janie's boots squeaked. She could see stable muck along their sides. There were voices from the upper hall. A sleek man appeared, carrying a swatch of fabric samples. He glanced toward Janie absently and looked beyond her. Behind him was Mrs. Cummings. She seemed almost to float down the stairs. Mrs. Cummings reminded Janie of a beautiful life-sized doll. She was never seen without her thick false eyelashes. She smelled of delicious flowers. Her pretty gown flowed around her. Janie looked at her admiringly.

"Why Janie, darling. A new summer here already! Isn't that wonderful! How's your dear mother? My, how you've grown. Yes, you have." Luckily she did not wait for a response. "Janie, this is Monsieur Pierre. He's helping me redecorate this old barn of a place." Monsieur Pierre looked bored.

"Andrea's new pony's here, Mrs. Cummings."

"Her what? Her pony?" Mrs. Cummings seemed confused. "How sweet. Why don't you pop up and see her?

She'll be just overjoyed to see one of her little friends again."

The long upstairs hall was lined with paintings in heavy frames. Stern faces looked out as Janie crept past. The doors were all closed. It was obvious that Andrea had no little brother like Janie's brother William to leave old clothes and dried-out frogs all over. She rapped at the last door and pushed it open. The sunlight was dazzling.

"Andrea . . ." Her voice broke off and she stared, mouth half open. A young woman sat on a ribboned cushion at Andrea's dressing table. Janie stood and watched as she carefully dabbed on lip gloss from a small gold jar. She patted the odd-looking dark red hair that hung to her shoulders. She regarded herself approvingly in the mirror,

smiling, her head tilted to one side. Finally she turned to Janie. It *was* Andrea. The smile vanished.

"Oh, it's only you, Janie." There was no note of welcome. The young woman looked Janie up and down slowly. "When are you going to start growing? Look at you!" She was amused. She returned to the mirror, lifted a red-tipped hand and flung a wig at Janie's feet. "It does absolutely nothing for me," she moaned. It was Andrea, all right. But not the same Andrea Janie had known last summer. Janie continued to examine her silently. It was hard to believe Andrea was only fourteen. She looked so grown-up. The silky pink robe gleamed as Andrea shook out her own light hair.

"Andrea, your pony's here." Janie hated her voice for sounding so childish. She cleared her throat and went on more firmly. "Pat said you should come and see him."

"Well, why didn't someone tell me? I'm never told anything around here." The light brown eyes were sulky now. Andrea gave one last glance at her reflection, frowned, and stood up. She swept out of the room, balanced on high satin slippers. Janie picked up the wig. She felt lumpy and sweaty. The frilly dressing table was crowded with jars, tiny boxes, ribbons. Janie saw her own flushed face in the mirror. Her hair stood out thick and curly. It looked like a nest. Her body was small, square and flat. Very flat. She wondered how it must feel to be Andrea. . . cool and grown-up.

Danny stood quietly as Pat removed his leg wrappings. He pricked his ears, swiveling them to catch the sounds of his new home. His neighbors, Noble and Milady, watched through the bars of their stalls while munching on their snacks of sweet meal and hay. Stable cats raced one another, eager to share the attention. Andrea slapped the crop against her suede chaps and looked at Danny. For a while nobody spoke.

"He's a good-looking animal," Pat said finally.

"But this kind of gray . . . it's so awfully ordinary." Andrea sounded cross.

"He's already won lots of prizes. Even a Grand Champion," Janie volunteered brightly.

"We-ell, I suppose he'll just have to do for now." Andrea was doubtful.

"He's really very intelligent, Andrea. Look at his eyes."

At last Andrea approached the pony. Danny sniffed her hand curiously, and she softened.

"Yes, I suppose he's quite sweet."

"Did you do much riding at school during the year, Andrea?" Pat was business-like. But Andrea avoided the question.

"Oh, they have such dreadful hacks at school. It's a waste of time to ride them."

"Well then, you have your summer's work mapped out for you. Your father has bought you a fine pony. That means he wants you to do well." Pat was firm. But Andrea pouted.

"Oh, that's Daddy. You'd think winning at horse shows was the same as making money with stocks and bonds. Anyway, I've just decided. I'm not going riding this morning after all. I'd rather go shopping with Mother. I haven't got a thing to wear."

With that, Andrea left. Pat and Janie looked at one another. Janie was speechless. How could Andrea leave without even trying Danny out?

9

Two

"William Neely, stop being such a pig!" Janie cried.

Mrs. Neely looked down from her perch on a kitchen stool. Her brown hair and blue eyes were the same as Janie's.

"Now, Janie. Don't be too hard on him. He's a growing boy," Mrs. Neely said.

William's plate was piled high. He had managed to spill scraps of food all around it. Janie thought he was revolting.

"That's right, Mom. Janie never understands." William made a face at his sister over the old cigar boxes and battered books in front of him. He was eager to defend himself. His eyes were round behind his glasses. He's probably still got half his breakfast stuck in his hair, Janie thought irritably, eyeing her brother's dark mop. He went on eating noisily. Janie vowed for the hundredth time to ignore him.

"Pat says Mr. Cummings paid an awful lot for Danny. But he's worth it. You can tell that just by looking at him," Janie went on to her mother.

"I'm afraid I've never known what to look for in horses," she replied lightly.

"Danny's not a horse. He's a pony!" William piped up importantly, trying for Janie's approval.

"I mean in ponies." But Mrs. Neely's mind was somewhere else. She was thinking about the college where she taught English. The summer term would be starting in a few days, and she wanted to get her housework out of the way while she had the chance. She was cleaning out the high kitchen cupboards, dressed in old jeans and a faded top. Janie watched her. Mrs. Neely looked quite young for a mother. But you could tell she was not really young by the creases under her eyes when she smiled. And she had a lot of silver hair coming through.

"Andrea is supposed to get ready for showing. She's going to have to work really hard getting Danny used to her," Janie explained. Mrs. Neely climbed down with a pile of old framed prints and a worn wooden box. She sensed Janie's mixed feelings.

"How is Andrea?" she asked.

"I couldn't really talk to her much." Janie was mumbling, embarrassed to admit to her mother how much her friend had changed. "Mrs. Cummings sent you her love. She's redecorating again!"

"Hmm . . . just like us!" Mrs. Neely stood with a print at arm's length trying to find a place to put it. Then, she opened the wooden box. "Look what I've found, Janie." Her face changed. "How you loved this photograph when you were small!"

Janie saw a handsome man on a black horse. William took a quick glimpse.

"That's Daddy, huh?" His mouth was full.

"Great looking fellow, wasn't he?" Mrs. Neely kept her voice light.

11

"Oh, yes. And look at his horse," Janie whispered. She hardly remembered her father.

"Janie, why don't you take it for your room?"

"Can I?" Janie was pleased.

William heaved himself up, pushing back his chair with a grating screech. He gathered up his cigar boxes and started for the door.

"So who's your servant, mister?" Janie's teeth were on edge. It was impossible to ignore him.

"I have to go and look for a new frog. Mine got lost today."

As usual, Mrs. Neely took his side. She ruffled his hair. "You do that, William."

William smirked at Janie triumphantly.

"But that doesn't mean tomorrow. *You* have to do the breakfast dishes tomorrow," Janie yelled after him.

Janie and her mother were at the sink when Janie realized her mother had something important to say. Her mind raced. What was it going to be? Would it be about William—the "be nice to your little brother because he has no father" speech? She hoped it wouldn't be "you're almost grown-up and there are things we must discuss." Janie hated her mother talking about things like that. It was much easier with Pat. And Pat knew everything.

"Janie," Mrs. Neely began as they cleared the table, "you go over to the Cummings' place a lot. Don't they mind?"

"Pat likes me to come over. She said so. I help her a lot."

"Janie." Mrs. Neely tried again. "Danny is Andrea's pony, not yours. You realize that, don't you? You and Andrea Cummings are two very different people."

That was true. Janie relaxed. "She's started wearing

12

makeup. And she was even trying on a wig," Janie giggled.

"Oh, my goodness." Mrs. Neely smiled as she ran water into the dish pan. "It's probably one of her mother's. She's growing up in a hurry." She handed some forks to Janie to dry. "Since Daddy died," Mrs. Neely went on, "there hasn't been much money to spare. You know that. Not for riding lessons. And certainly not for a pony."

"I never even thought of having a pony," Janie said uneasily, wondering if all mothers could read minds. "But I do love to ride, and Pat's been giving me pointers for a long time now. She says I'm getting to be a good rider."

"That's great. But you're just the girl from down the road. Andrea's the one getting ready for a horse show." Mrs. Neely hesitated, her hands still for a moment. "It's just that I don't want my daughter envying anyone. Do you understand what I'm trying to say?"

Janie looked away guiltily. And then the phone rang, breaking the tension. It was Pat. Janie began to smile as she listened, and then put her hand over the receiver.

"Mom! Andrea's taking Danny out for his first workout this afternoon. Can I go over? Please say yes!"

"But you know today was to be clean-up day." Janie's smile faded.

William had just returned, and stood in the doorway.

"How about you helping me?" Mrs. Neely asked.

William sized up the situation. He smiled good-naturedly.

"Okay. But then I'll need some pitching practice, Mom. I'm really bad."

Mrs. Neely shook her head, laughing at the trap.

13

"All right, William. That's a bargain." She looked at Janie and spoke softly. "Now remember what I said, Janie. Your life is going to be very different from Andrea's."

"I'll remember, Mom." Janie began to leave. Then she turned back. "Thanks, William." He grinned at her happily.

Three

Janie squirmed in the hot sun. Danny's mane and tail flew as he trotted past. Andrea wore her new tan chaps and a dark velvet helmet. She was thinner than last summer, Janie noticed.

"He's fighting me. He's not even trying," Andrea complained loudly.

"It's his first workout. A new place and a new rider. And you're handling him badly." Pat was patient. Janie squinted as she watched. Pat nearly always wore old jeans and a shirt. So did Janie. Pat often wore a scarf to keep her hair neat. So did Janie. Pat liked to wear beat-up work boots every day. So did Janie. Andrea's shirt was silk. And her new field boots were soft and smooth.

Danny was cantering now. Andrea was managing him better. But the pony became skittish. His nostrils flared and he danced wide at the turn. Andrea lashed at him with her crop. He whinnied and tossed his head.

"You've got to control him, Andrea. And that's not the way to do it." Pat's voice had sharpened. Andrea pulled the pony up, dragging angrily at his mouth. She flung down the reins and glared at Pat. Just then a cat flashed across the ring. The stable dog saw it and set off, yapping, in pursuit. Danny was startled. He jerked his head, reared

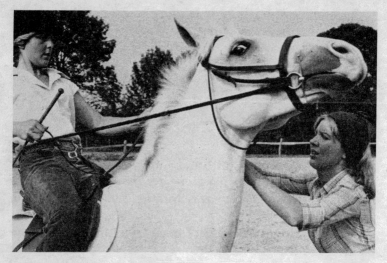

back and was off, racing to the far end of the ring with a terrified Andrea clinging to his mane. Janie felt her knees go weak.

Pat moved quickly. She ran to intercept the pony. Janie caught up with them as Pat slowed Danny, hanging on to his reins, forcing him to stop. The three of them gasped while Danny snorted. He bucked and blustered, but Pat held him firmly. Then he quieted and hung his head. It's as if he's ashamed, Janie thought. Andrea jumped down, her face red. She stepped toward Danny's head and lifted her crop high.

"Don't you ever do that, Andrea!" Pat grabbed her arm. Andrea glared at her and stomped off.

"Andrea . . ." Janie began.

"Let her go, Janie." Pat's voice trembled. "Well, Danny is a touchy fellow. You'd better walk him a bit and then take him back to his stall."

The stable was quiet and pleasantly musty. Janie attached the crossties and took off Danny's tack. She sponged his sweat-stained back. He thrust his nose into her hair. "No need to tell me you're sorry," she whispered. "We are your friends here, you know." By the time Pat came in he was cool and fresh again. "Pat, I'm sure he'll never do that again," Janie said. "He was just nervous. Everything was so new."

"Maybe. Or maybe he's not what we expected. You know, Janie, a horse or pony can win every ribbon around. Then suddenly everything can go wrong." She looked at Danny thoughtfully. "I just hope Mr. Cummings hasn't made a mistake. Now don't look so gloomy! Why don't you take old Noble for his exercise and leave this fellow to me?" Janie gave Danny one final pat and left.

The big dun Noble enjoyed cantering across the ring and down the trails. He was docile and affectionate. One of Janie's favorites. A pair of horses whinnied jealously from their paddock.

"Your turn tomorrow," she promised as she passed. Riding was better than just about anything else in the world, Janie thought. There was not one horse at Longvue she hadn't learned to handle well. Except Danny, of course. He was a pony, she reminded herself. Maybe she'd get a chance to ride him soon. She thought of his white mane and tail flying as he galloped. Like something out of a fairy tale. If only he hadn't bolted like that.

"Hey, Janie." Pat called her out of her daydream. Janie rode over to her. Noble twitched a muscle and flicked his tail skillfully against the flies. He looked around politely, as if to ask why they had stopped. Pat shaded her eyes with a strong, sunburned hand as Janie dismounted.

17

"I've been talking with Mr. Cummings. About Danny. Andrea won't be able to train him herself and he'll need special attention I won't have time to give him. How would you like to help get him ready for the next show?"

"You mean it? THAT'S GREAT!"

"You'll be paid for your work. It's not much, but it's something. Mr. Cummings thinks it will be good for Andrea to have someone her own age here all the time. So now you're officially part of the Longvue workforce." She slapped Noble easily and he gave her a gentle nudge in return.

Mrs. Neely was in the kitchen when Janie burst in to tell her the good news.

"That's lovely, Janie. I'm really pleased for you. And I know you'll do a great job. Now, listen dear. Will you go get changed? I've still got a big batch of papers to grade, and then I could use your help. Mr. De Vito is coming to dinner."

"Oh, him! Why is he always coming over?" Janie's voice was hostile.

"Because he's a friend. And it would really help if you'd try to be nice. Okay?"

Janie brushed her hair as flat as she could. No good. It just popped up again. Why couldn't she wait and take her shower before bed like she always did? It was silly to get two sets of clothes all dirty for no reason. Just because of a bit of horse sweat. It was Mr. De Vito's fault, of course. She went downstairs.

Mrs. Neely was preparing the salad, and William sat

looking at a picture in a magazine with Mike De Vito. Janie started to arrange the flowers as her mother had asked. She watched them scornfully as she worked. Her mother was all dressed up. She had pulled her hair back. And she had put on lipstick and rouge. Her eyes looked especially bright. William was worst of all. He acts as if Mike is some movie actor, or the president of the United States, Janie thought. He was nauseating.

"Mike, do you think my caterpillar will turn into one of those?" William knew quite well that those butterflies in the magazine came from Africa. But Mike treated him as though he was the most brilliant kid who ever walked the earth. As for Mike De Vito, Janie had to admit there was nothing really bad about him. He just did not fit in here. For one thing, he was always going on about Texas. Just because he had lived there for a while, he spoke like a Texan half the time. William thought that was just great. And Mike loved old Western movies. The kind you saw late at night, if you were allowed up. Or on wet Sunday afternoons. In fact, he was talking right now as if he was a real Texas cowboy. Janie turned and challenged him.

"Did you ever learn to ride a horse, Mr. De Vito?"

"Funny you should ask now, Janie." He gave her an easy smile. "Would you believe it? I went to a dude ranch once. Yup! And while I was there I actually climbed all the way up onto a horse! That's when I bought my ten-gallon hat. And my lizard boots. Ever notice my fancy boots, William?" He lifted a lanky leg while William watched, wide-eyed. Janie knew he was teasing her, but she could not stop.

"That does *not* mean you can ride a horse. Mr. Cum-

19

mings over at Longvue doesn't have a ten-gallon hat. And he doesn't wear Western boots. He only wears English riding clothes."

Mike refused to get annoyed. "Sounds like a lovely man."

"And he's very rich," Janie went on recklessly. "They own three homes and four horses. And now Danny." At that Mrs. Neely broke in.

"Having lots of money has nothing to do with whether Mr. Cummings is a nice man or not," she snapped. Janie's cheeks burned. She tried again.

"Mr. Cummings has hired me to help get Danny ready for showing."

"That a fact? Must mean you're pretty good, Janie." Mr. De Vito sounded really pleased for her. Then William had to chime in.

"Andrea doesn't like Danny. She thinks he's a lemon. I heard her say so."

"That's not so. He was nervous today, that's all. He's a beautiful pony."

"And a lucky one as well, I'd say. Having a friend like you," Mike answered. Janie looked away quickly.

William reached down under his chair. He pulled up an old baseball glove, worn from years of use. "Mike, after dinner, will you let me throw a ball to you? I really need some practice."

Mike took the glove and tried it on, punching it with his fist. "Now this is one fine glove."

"That's my father's glove," Janie snapped rudely before she could stop herself. "Isn't it, Mom?"

Mrs. Neely did not answer. Janie felt miserable. She started for the stairs.

"Janie." Mrs. Neely called her back. "I'd like you to help set the table." Mike held up a hand, grinning amiably.

"Hold on there. I may not be much on a horse. But I'm first rate at setting tables."

Upstairs Janie looked at the photograph on her mirror. The handsome man on a fine horse had been her father.

"Dude ranch!" she muttered. "Westerns! Huh!"

Four

Two weeks had passed. Janie held a lunge-line. She turned on the spot while Danny circled at the end of the lead. He was frisky today. Janie had to work hard to keep him moving properly. Even so she could see Andrea and another girl lounging at the ringside. Farther away Pat was loading a wheelbarrow with sawdust and wheeling it into the stable. Andrea's friend was tall and languid. She flipped back her straight hair with long pale fingers. Her nails were dark red. Andrea's nails were even longer and darker.

"So that's the famous new pony, is it?" The friend sounded bored.

"Oh, he's just for this year. I'm already growing out of him. Father's talking of getting me a Thoroughbred for next season."

When Danny had had enough, Janie looped up the line and led him to the gate. She patted him, receiving a sweet nuzzle as she walked. She paused in front of the two older girls.

Andrea finally spoke.

"This is Janie, Betty. She's here to help get the pony

ready for showing. And he's going to need an awful lot of help."

"He's moving just beautifully, Andrea," Janie protested. "Ask Pat. Aren't you going to ride at all today?"

Both girls ignored Janie.

"Do you really think he'll be ready for the Hungerford Show?" Betty sounded doubtful.

"He'd better be!" Andrea shot Janie a hard look.

"He will be, Andrea. Just wait and see," Janie promised. But the two of them had turned their backs.

"Come on, Betty. Let's go up to the house. I want you to see my new riding outfit. It's gorgeous!" Janie watched

them wander off, picking their way carefully in their delicate sandals. Pat called from close by. "This is my last load, thank goodness. Just cool Danny out. Then I want you to come up to the cottage with me."

Janie smiled at her gratefully. "Okay," she replied, feeling more cheerful. Pat was more fun than Andrea, anyway.

"Yoohoo! Pat! Janie!" Mrs. Cummings waved to them. She drifted across the lawn. Next to her a serious young man held his pencil poised over an open notebook. "Hello, girls. This is dear Mr. Muller. He's helping me find a way to make all of this"—she gestured helplessly—"a little less . . . er . . . ordinary!" Mrs. Cummings posed prettily next to a garden sculpture. She was thinking. Then, "Now, Mr. Muller. What would you say to a rock garden? Yes, that's it, a Japanese rock garden. Right here!" She pointed triumphantly with her toe to the thick lawn in front of her. Mr. Muller nodded solemnly. Pat and Janie exchanged grins and continued on their way.

Pat's cottage was tiny. It had its own little porch. Inside was a pleasant mixture of old and not-so-old furniture, bright cushions, plants and pictures. The day bed was unmade. Books lay everywhere. On the wall were some framed photographs.

"Pat, I never knew you rode in the Garden." Pat had been so young then, Janie noticed.

"Oh, those! Don't look at the year. It sure dates me!" Pat moved swiftly. "See? One of the best things about living on your own. You make your bed when you feel like it." She threw the cushions into place.

"When I have my own house, it's going to be just like this."

"Why thank you, Janie. But I'm not going to win any prizes for interior decorating with it. Let's have a soda, shall we?" Janie sat carefully on a basket chair while Pat opened Cokes. She handed one to Janie, and flopped onto the couch.

"Whew! That's better." Pat raised her Coke in the air. "I propose a toast. To you, Janie and to the whole wonderful, crazy world of horses you've just come into." The two of them drank thirstily. "You're really part of it, now that you'll be working with Danny. And, Janie, there are two kinds of people in that world." She drank again. "Some care most about winning, and about glamour, fancy clothes, being admired, being part of the smart set. The others are different. They love horses and ponies. No matter what or where."

"Even Western?" Janie ventured.

"That's right, even Western! And work horses, young horses, old horses—and ponies. The true horse lover will work for them, care for them, love them." She paused. "End of lecture." Pat smiled and lifted her glass again. "Another toast. To Longvue Farm and the even more wonderful place it will become. If Mrs. Cummings ever gets finished redecorating it!"

"And to Danny?"

"And to Danny!"

"You're doing beautifully, Andrea. Now let's try him on some fences." Danny took up his trot and whinnied as if he knew he looked handsome. That morning Janie had bathed him and she watched proudly as he passed. Even Andrea seemed pleased. Danny took all six fences without hesitation.

"Not bad at all. Keep going. Give him a little more leg." Pat was not going to let Andrea relax. "That was better. But you've got a long way to go."

Mr. Cummings was strolling over from the house. Mrs. Cummings clung to his arm, holding onto a huge red floppy hat that matched her dress. Andrea let her parents admire her jumping and then rode over and dismounted. "How did I look?" she asked eagerly.

Mrs. Cummings sounded distressed. "Darling, that lovely embroidered blouse. I bought it for you to wear at the party. Isn't there anything else you could have put

on?" Andrea took off her helmet and glanced down impatiently. She dusted off her sleek breeches.

"Oh, Mother! What does it matter? How did I look?" She repeated to her father.

"Looked pretty good to me. But I won't be doing the judging. Now, listen to me young lady. I don't approve of doing things in halves. It's not going to be like last year. You're going to give this your full concentration, aren't you?"

"Yes."

"You see, my dear, it's very simple. There are winners and there are losers. If you want to ride you must make up your mind. You are a winner! Agreed?"

Andrea sighed. "Agreed."

"Oh, Monty, you make it all sound so frightfully serious," Mrs. Cummings said to her husband.

Mr. Cummings turned to Pat. "What do you think, Pat? Is the pony ready to show?"

"Only one way to find out. And that's to try," Pat replied.

"Good. We'll do it." He put an arm each around his wife and daughter and they strolled off.

Danny ambled back to the paddock, his head bobbing next to Janie's. "Now you see, Danny," she told him, "you did just as you were told. You worked hard. And now you're going to be showing. Isn't that great?"

Five

It was just after dawn that July morning when Pat led a drowsy Danny out of his stall. The other horses neighed noisily.

"I know, little fellow, you'd much rather sleep." She laughed aloud as Danny perked up at the sight of the trailer. "Oh, so that made you wake up fast. Yes, you're going on an outing."

The sky was streaked with pink and birds were chattering in the tall trees when Janie and Andrea appeared.

"I shouldn't have to send Janie to wake you up, Andrea," Pat said.

"I had a date last night. Do you mind?"

"You don't date the night before a show. Anyway, you're too young."

"You date, so why shouldn't I?"

"Because I'm not thirteen. Now hurry, there's lots to do."

Andrea slammed the jeep door. "I'm fourteen," she muttered.

Janie crept into the back. Andrea's new riding oufit had been thrown across the seat beside her. Janie felt the velvet helmet. She straightened the dark blue jacket, and smoothed the pale leather gloves. The big day had begun.

Janie was hollow with anxiety. She had also forgotten to eat breakfast.

The Hungerford show ground was filling fast when they reached it. Trailer ramps were down and folding chairs set out. Everyone seemed busy. Bridles and bits were soaped and polished. Boots and jackets were brushed. Janie stared wide-eyed. She had never seen so many horses and ponies. All colors, all sizes, they neighed and fretted, eager to begin. Hooves were picked clean. Faces were wiped. Tails tied up. Danny lifted his head and snorted a greeting, shaking himself awake. A dainty strawberry roan picked up the call. Two white-faced ponies shook their dark manes and kicked at their van sides. A dun gelding turned to join in, but his rider quickly called him to order.

Janie listened to the distant burst of applause from the rings. Classes were announced over loudspeakers. Mounts were schooled before they competed. Janie breathed in the smells of wet grass, soap and horses. There were hamburgers and hot dogs broiling in the striped food tent. She wanted to laugh out loud from the joy of being here. Instead she concentrated on giving Danny's tack a last rub.

A grimy kid was staring at her. His hair was limp, his pale eyes tired.

"What do you want?" Janie asked gruffly after a few moments.

"Nothing. Just thought maybe I could help. Or something."

"You can bring that bucket here if you like." Danny drank noisily and the boy looked pleased. He stroked the pony's head, looking up at him admiringly. Suddenly he left. Pat was coming.

"Who's your friend?"

"Him? He's not my friend. I don't even know him!" Janie replied indignantly. But she saw the pale face peering from the crowd several times that day.

Andrea appeared at the stall dressed in her riding habit. She pulled back irritably when Pat straightened the number on her back.

"Darling, you look adorable, just adorable," Mrs. Cummings burbled as she walked past.

"Remember, Andrea. I want a blue ribbon," Mr. Cummings reminded her loudly.

"No matter what he gets, Janie, you made Danny the best-looking pony in the show," Pat murmured. Janie glowed with pride.

Riders and their mounts waited quietly at the ring entrance. When the signal to begin was given, they lined up to receive their instructions. They would walk, trot and canter in this equitation class. Points would be given for overall appearance as well as for riding skills. How beautiful they looked, Janie thought, as the twenty riders and their mounts circled the ring. But Pat was not pleased.

"Now that's what I call sloppy riding."

Janie craned to see where Andrea was making her mistakes.

"Andrea's riding very badly today." Mr. Cummings' clipped accent carried from the far side of the ring. Andrea tightened her mouth.

"But, darling, she's having such a good time." Mrs. Cummings protested.

"She did not come here to have a good time," Mr. Cummings added coldly. "She came here to win."

Andrea was not called to stand among the lead riders at the end of the class. She rode out of the ring. Her face was stormy. She tossed the reins to Janie and stalked off. Janie heard her explain laughingly to her friends that Danny was badly trained. And he simply was not good enough for her.

The show grew more festive. Stalls were piled high with souvenirs. Friends and relatives arrived to encourage favorites. Janie's stomach rumbled. She promised herself she would listen to Pat in the future and never, never leave for a show on an empty stomach. When the two of them finally ate, Janie swore it was the most delicious hamburger of her whole life.

Pat and Janie chose a good spot to watch the hunter class. If only Danny would do well for this one, Janie prayed silently. The first rider took three fences elegantly. But then his brown mare knocked two rails off and he seemed to lose control. Pat and Janie shook their heads in sympathy as he rode out. The next two entries seemed first class to Janie's inexperienced eyes. Andrea's friend, Betty, rode in on her roan Thoroughbred. The onlookers clapped and whooped at her last round. Andrea was next. Danny trotted out gallantly. But there was trouble right away.

"She's pulling him too much. He's not going to like this." Pat was angry.

The first jumps were not bad. Danny balked at the third. Andrea lashed him with her crop. He stumbled and whinnied in protest. She circled him for a new approach. Faults were piling up. Janie held her breath as they reached the jump. Sure enough, he ran around the jump, refusing to take it. And as he swerved, Andrea lost her hold and fell. There was a gasp and a moment of silence. Danny stood still, looking back. Andrea lay still. Mrs. Cummings clung to her husband's sleeve, her hand at her mouth. But Andrea rose, looked down at her soiled jodhpurs and grabbed Danny's reins.

Pat and Janie ran to catch up as Andrea dragged Danny away. Pat was furious.

"Next time you fall off a horse, you get up and get on again. You finish the course. You're not hurt."

"This pony is just no good." Andrea was bitter.

"Darling, are you all right? Oh, you poor sweetheart," Mrs. Cummings panted in distress.

"Pat, we didn't get a pony. We got a lemon." Mr. Cummings looked at Danny with contempt. Janie's heart pounded and her eyes stung.

Pat and Janie rode home alone in the jeep, a tired Danny in the van behind.

"Why did Danny do that?" Janie asked miserably.

"Horses and people, Janie. They have one thing in common. You never quite know what they'll do next. Maybe he just needs more work. Maybe he felt like acting up against the sloppy way Andrea was handling him. Or maybe," she paused and grew serious. "Maybe he *is* a lemon."

Six

Next day the stable chores were finished early. Now Janie waited glumly on Pat's small porch. She watched the party preparations from a distance. Long tables had been set up on the lawns. Uniformed servers hurried back and forth from the lawn to the house. Music filtered softly through the trees. It was a perfect day for a party. But Janie picked moodily at the lace trim of her sleeve. Pat was so lucky, she decided. She never had to get dressed up. Except for jodhpurs on really special occasions. Janie frowned as she smoothed her long red and white skirt. She reached up and felt the thin ribbon holding her hair. She was going to feel awfully stupid walking down there in this get-up. And Pat wearing anything she wanted to. She stretched out a foot. They were nice sandals. She had chosen them. But she'd rather wear work boots any day.

A group of guests arrived, laughing and chatting as they walked up the drive. Some kids chased each other across the garden. One boy dived under a table, hiding behind the long tablecloth. A small girl searched for him. Janie had not played games like that for ages. It had been fun being a little kid. Janie gave a long weary sigh. The door behind her opened.

Pat announced herself. "Ta-da!" she sang out. Janie's

spirits dropped even further. It wasn't just the hair which was piled up high with tendrils curling over her ears and neck. It wasn't even the makeup which hid Pat's freckles and made her face glow. It was just that she didn't look like Pat anymore.

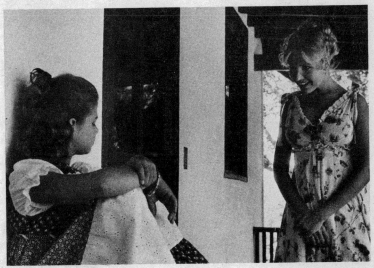

"Well? What do you say?" Pat laughed at her little friend's face. "Okay, I'll answer for you. Fantastic! Unbelievable!" She took Janie's arm and led her gaily from the porch. "Come on. Let's have some fun."

As soon as they reached the terrace, Janie knew she had lost Pat. Everyone seemed to know her and to want to speak to her. Anyway, Janie reminded herself sternly, I'm proud of her. She is pretty. And she's nice, too. But deep down Janie felt lonely. The long buffet tables were piled high. Skewered meats and chicken were browning on the grill. But Janie had no appetite.

Janie passed huge pots of flowering shrubs. There were piles of dark cherries heaped on flat wicker trays. She took a cherry, but her stomach felt like a lump of lead. Mrs. Cummings stood, cool and charming, at the top of some stone steps.

"Hello, Janie, dear," she called out. "Isn't your mother here yet? I hope she's bringing her friend. I hear he is fascinating!"

Janie wove her way among the tables. Ahead a tall young man in a light suit was looking around eagerly. His face lit up as he strode toward Janie and then past her. She turned to watch. The strange young man had seen Pat. He put his arms around her and bent to kiss her cheek. Pat looked up at him happily. Janie wandered around the house. Below on a flagged terrace, Andrea was teaching a group of teenagers a new dance. Their transistor radio beat a steady rhythm. Andrea wore something silky and sophisticated. The skirt swung as she danced on spiky sandals. Janie looked down at her own small feet. Her cotton dress with its puffed sleeves looked childish, she knew. Andrea glanced up at Janie's gloomy face and muttered to her friends. They stared. "Who's your cute friend, Andrea?" Someone smirked. Janie lifted her chin and walked away.

When Janie first saw the three figures walking up the drive, she felt better. Her mother wore a linen caftan. Her hair was loose. William had on his best suit. He still clutched his old cigar boxes. Mike De Vito was there too. He introduced himself and Mrs. Neely to a group of guests. He's not even shy, Janie thought. And yet look

36

how he was dressed! Not just his fancy shirt with the Western tie at the neck. But on his head was a huge white felt ten-gallon hat, which he tipped in greeting. Her mother looked up at him lovingly. As for William, he hung onto Mike as though he were his real father. Janie found herself a solitary seat under a hedge and sat there simmering.

Janie watched crossly as her mother and Mike De Vito stood in a corner of the garden close by. They had not seen her and they stared contentedly over the valley to the river.

"The South Side of Chicago was never like this," Mike said.

"Neither was Poughkeepsie." Kate laughed. They seemed to have a private joke. They looked at each other.

"Kate. Oh, Kate." Vicky Cummings chirped sweetly as she bore down on them. "Kate darling, you look adorable. Just adorable." She turned to Mike. "Mr. De Vito! I have been hearing interesting stories about you. You're a builder!" She said it as though it were something fantastic.

"A contractor, ma'am." Mike looked amused. Vicky threw out her arms extravagantly.

"And that wonderful costume you're wearing!"

Mike put on the drawl Janie had grown to hate.

"Mrs. Cummings, ma'am. This is no costume. These are my Western threads."

Mr. Cummings strode over and took his wife's arm. "Come along, Vicky. They've started on desserts." He looked at Mike coldly.

"Monty, have you met Kate's charming friend, Mr. De Vito?" The two men nodded at one another.

Mr. Cummings smiled boyishly at Mrs. Neely.

"Kate, your Janie is just a priceless jewel. That is my considered opinion." Janie was surprised.

"A bit uncut and unpolished, I'm afraid," Kate laughed.

"But a beauty like her mother, nonetheless," Mike added. "Happy birthday to you, Mr. Cummings."

"Why, thank you. Now come along my dear." He steered Vicky away. "If you will excuse us."

The party dragged on for Janie. She heard rolls of distant thunder and thought of the animals in the stables. They all hated storms, Danny most of all. She smiled as she recalled how he had nuzzled up to her when she sat in his stall waiting out the last one. She could not stop the cracks of lightning or the deafening thunder. But he seemed less afraid with her there. If only she could sneak out now and go down to the stable.

Kate Neely and Mike De Vito sat among a group of

guests on the far side of the lawn. A woman played the guitar and sang. She sang about love and loneliness, and about farewells. Janie edged closer and felt a lump come into her throat. They all seemed to share the same secret her mother and Mike had. As if they were in a magic spell. All except William. He was being himself, yawning, trapping insects with his hands and letting them run over his mother's skirt. Mrs. Neely looked up at Janie and patted the ground next to her. Grudgingly, Janie accepted the invitation. The song ended. There was a long silence. Everyone was lost in dreams. Then Mike spoke out in his deep voice.

"Now how about a song from the old West?" The singer thought, and then picked out some notes. It was "Streets of Laredo." She sang a few bars and then Mike joined in. His voice was pleasant. He finished the song alone. Kate watched him in a way that made Janie squirm. Everyone clapped. Except Janie.

"I really do love those old Western ballads," he said, almost to himself. Janie was quick to attack.

"But you're from Chicago." Her voice was scornful, cutting through the chatter. There was an awkward silence. Mrs. Neely flushed. Mike was not disturbed. He waited, a lazy smile warming his face as he looked at Janie.

"Ah, yes, Janie. Even in Chicago we had our dreams. Just as you have yours." Janie glared at him. And slowly her anger faded. She remembered her own special dream about Danny, and her dark blue eyes softened.

It was twilight as the four of them walked home across the meadow. Janie stayed next to her mother, but William clung to Mike.

"Where did you find him? Such a fabulous man!" Kate Neely imitated Mrs. Cummings mischievously. Janie felt relaxed.

"Did you notice our Janie? She made a conquest." Mike wanted to include her, she knew.

"Yuk! He was a creep!" But Janie smiled to herself as she remembered the earnest boy in braces who followed her around toward the end of the party. "Did you see Andrea?" she asked. "She was smoking behind the house." Her voice rose.

"I hardly recognized her." Mrs. Neely answered. "She has changed." They reached the old barn-red cottage which was their home. Kate unlocked the door and gave William a gentle shove.

"You, young man, are taking a bath and heading for bed."

"I wanna watch television," he whined.

"Not tonight." Kate was firm. "Janie, will you make sure he gets to bed? He'll take forever." Janie followed her sleepy brother into the house.

"I can get my own self ready," he protested. Janie was thinking back over the party. There was something she forgot to tell her mother. She looked back out the door. Kate and Mike were not there. Janie peered around the door and stepped out. They were next to the old brick well in the garden. She stopped and stared, the strangest feelings coming up into her stomach and chest. Mike had his arms around Kate. And he was kissing her! It lasted and lasted. Janie looked at them in horror. Her eyes smarted.

"I hate him! I hate him!" she raged. And she slammed the door shut with all her might.

Seven

When Janie was riding, nothing seemed bad. Sure enough, the next day's workout brought a better mood. There was the old familiar Pat in comfortable jeans and boots. Danny's mane flew in front of Janie as she galloped, and his tack was as shiny as she could make it. She moved easily on the pony.

"Okay, Janie," Pat called. "Nice work. He's coming along. Keep that pace." Janie was even more determined now. She slowed Danny and wheeled him around to approach the jumps. She leaned over and patted his smooth pearly neck. His big ears perked up as she spoke to him.

"Danny, I want you to do your very best. Do it for me, Danny." He pulled up his head. Danny was ready. Janie put him into a canter and headed for the first jump. He cleared it without hesitation. Why couldn't he have done that at the show? Janie wondered.

"Great, Janie. Keep going," Pat yelled. Once again Janie circled. But this time she took him over all six fences. She rode over to Pat, her face shining.

"See, Pat. There's nothing at all wrong with his jumping."

"That's what it looks like. Go and get Andrea, Janie. I want her to see how he's doing today. She should be back on him getting some training. He's got to work with the one who'll be showing him."

Moments later Janie was racing across the lawn to the Cummings' house. All signs of the party had been cleared away. The house was as peaceful as ever. Janie could smell coffee brewing. But there was no sound of anyone downstairs. She tiptoed up to Andrea's room. The door was open. Andrea's voice came from inside. Janie tapped and then entered the room.

Andrea was stretched across her bed, leaning on a pile of tiny ribboned pillows. She held a pink telephone to her ear.

"He's really quite a darling. He called me this morning first thing." Andrea saw Janie standing hot and rumpled inside the door. She waved limply and turned away.

"I suppose he wants to show me how very well brought up he is. So, of course he said all the proper things." She looked at Janie again and rolled her eyes heavenward in exasperation. "Just a minute."

"Well. What do you want?" she demanded rudely.

"Pat said you should come and ride Danny. He's completely changed. You should see the way he's been jumping," Janie said.

Andrea pursed her narrow mouth and thought. Then, "You can tell Pat that I don't care. I don't want to ride him now . . . or ever!" She looked back at the telephone. "And Betty, you'll never guess what! He tried to kiss me!" She burst into gales of laughter. Janie closed the door behind her, but not before she heard Andrea's voice continue. "Oh, but he's so clumsy. Do you know what he did? . . ."

Danny was waiting patiently in his stall when Janie stormed back into the stable. He followed her with his large, intelligent eyes. Janie kissed his soft pink nose, and looked lovingly at him. Why didn't Andrea care? Well, no matter what, Danny needed his training. She led him back out again.

Pat was already in the ring on Milady, Mrs. Cummings' chestnut mare. Pat rode so well. One day, Janie decided, she would ride as well as Pat. Danny was dragging back on the reins. Janie turned to encourage him, and something seemed to lurch painfully in her. She bent down to look. Then she walked him a few steps.

"Pat! Pat! Come quickly, please. It's Danny. He's hurt his leg. He's lame!"

Eight

Dr. Greaves, the veterinarian, examined Danny thoroughly. He bent the left front foot again and let it drop to the ground. His forehead creased as he spoke.

"Maybe that's why he balked at the show. He might have been in pain." Mr. Cummings nodded impatiently. "I don't think it's a fracture," Dr. Greaves went on. "But I'll need to take some X rays." He passed his hand carefully over the leg and shoulder. Danny's skin twitched. Mr. Cummings curled his lip in irritation.

"A lame horse is no better than one with a broken leg as far as I'm concerned," he said.

Pat held Danny's halter firmly. "What kind of treatment should he get?" she asked Dr. Greaves.

"That depends on what I find in the X rays. But I'd say hosing down every few hours. And lots of care."

"I could do that." Janie's voice was pleading. No one answered her. Dr. Greaves replaced the instruments in his sagging black bag.

"I'll be by later for those X rays." He sounded calm. But Mr. Cummings' eyes flicked over the pony scornfully.

"What are the chances of this animal ever being any good for showing? Isn't once lame always lame?" he demanded. Dr. Greaves shrugged his shoulders. A rumble of thunder overhead made the horses start and kick restlessly. Lightning and more thunder followed.

There was the sound of running, and Andrea slipped into the stable. She looked delicate in a blue slicker. She posed at the door, playing the helpless little girl for her father and Dr. Greaves. She reached out to Danny. "Poor baby," she murmured. Danny eyed her quietly at first. Then he reared back unexpectedly, pulling up his head, startling them all. Andrea tightened her mouth and stalked out into the downpour. Janie held Danny's bridle. It must have been the thunder. But Mr. Cummings nodded to himself and turned to the veterinarian.

"Thanks a lot, Doc. I'll wait for your report then." He paused at the door and looked up into the dark skies. "Pat, will you come up to the house later? I want to talk to you." The men left together.

Janie held her face close to Danny's as though she could somehow take over his pain.

"It was all my fault, Pat. I asked him to jump. He did it for me. And now he's hurt."

Pat looked at her wearily. There was nothing left to say.

"Why don't you go home now, Janie. The rain's letting up. Everything's done here. Danny will be getting his X rays. Then we'll know more."

Janie dragged herself home.

Nine

The next day, Janie really did not want to go on the picnic. But her mother insisted. Mike and William raced around in their own kind of football. Mrs. Neely lay on the big blanket, enjoying the break from work. But Janie sat bleakly watching dragonflies dancing above a small pond. The food had been eaten. Janie wanted to leave.

"Andrea doesn't care," she complained. "He's her pony and he's in pain. That's why he limps. She doesn't care."

Her mother groaned. Her dreams of a peaceful family afternoon were fading fast.

"Janie, we're all here together and we want to have a good time. I wish you'd forget that horse. Just this once."

"He's a pony. I should be back there. Dr. Greaves will have the results on the X rays. Anyway, Danny needs to be hosed down."

"Then Andrea should be doing it. He *is* her pony," Mrs. Neely flashed back.

"I know he's hers. Everyone is always telling me that. But it's my job to take care of him. I'm being paid to do it."

"Here we come! Straight for the goal . . . ." There was a flurry of activity and Mike threw himself onto the blanket. William rushed after him, face flushed, hair standing in spikes. He flung himself next to Mike.

"Touchdown! Touchdown!" Mike looked at Mrs. Neely. He bent forward and gently kissed her forehead. William grinned at them. Like a complete little idiot, Janie thought irritably.

"William, that was a good game. Well fought. And well played." Mike returned Janie's look calmly. "Guess you're not in any mood for all this silly fooling around, huh?" He seemed so understanding that in place of her annoyance, Janie felt her throat fill and her eyes sting. She ducked her head. Mrs. Neely rescued her.

"Well, we tried. But I don't think our Janie is going to forget that pony. Not even for a minute." She stood up.

Mike drove home past Longvue Farm to drop off Janie. Danny was in his stall as though nothing had changed. Janie saw that he kept his weight carefully on three legs. She scratched his ears and he leaned close to her.

"Don't you worry, Danny. I'm going to take care of you. And you're going to get all better, fast." He rubbed his face against her, snuffling at the side of her neck until she laughed. "Now take it easy. I know you love me. But you don't have to knock me down to tell me so."

Moments later Janie was tapping on Pat's door. "It's just me, Pat." A record was playing folk music. Pat stood at the table sorting her clean laundry.

"These jeans!" she exclaimed. "You'd think by now I should take them out and bury them. I mean they've done a full job and earned a rest. But I ask you, when do I have time to go to a store and buy new ones?"

"When I grow up," Janie declared, "I'm going to be just like you. I'm never going to get married." Pat looked startled. She smiled.

"Janie, you have me figured all wrong."

"No one tells you what to do. You're your own boss."

"And Mr. Cummings. Who's he may I ask?"

"You know what I mean, Pat. You don't have to . . ." Janie made a face. "My mother thinks Mr. De Vito is just wonderful."

"I think he's pretty nice myself." Pat spoke quietly. Then she turned and looked at Janie, with a serious expression on her face. "Janie. There's something unpleasant we have to talk about. Try not to be too upset. Mr. Cummings spoke to me today."

"About Danny?" Janie asked.

"I'm afraid so. Dr. Greaves has advised Mr. Cummings to get rid of Danny."

No, no! Janie hardly knew what she did next. She looked around wildly, leaped up and ran out the door.

"Janie. Janie." Pat caught up with her on the grass out-

side the main house. Janie was on her knees, sobbing bitterly. "Listen, Janie. You said you want to be like me. That means you want to make a living caring for horses. Okay. Then the most important thing you have to accept is the fact that horses and ponies are going to come and go. You do your best. That's all."

"But Danny is special. He jumped because I asked him to. He did it for me, even if it hurt him. It was my fault."

"Now listen, Janie. He had an old injury or a weakness there. That's why. Try and understand. Danny is not just a pet for Andrea. He's meant to ride, and to win."

"I'll take care of Danny." Janie was begging now. "I'll hose down his leg. I'll . . ."

Without stopping to think, Janie stormed into the Cummings' house. Pat trailed behind her.

49

Mr. Cummings looked up from his newspaper.

"Yes, Janie?"

Janie took a deep breath to calm herself. "Mr. Cummings, it's about Danny. Please don't let him go. You don't have to pay me. I'll work really hard to make his leg better. Please, Mr. Cummings?" Her face was tearstained as she gazed passionately at him.

"Didn't Pat tell you?" he began. But Janie interrupted.

"He'll be able to go to shows again soon, Mr. Cummings. I know he will."

"Then you know something Dr. Greaves doesn't. There's no way of knowing whether that pony will ever be any good again."

Janie appealed to Pat. "Pat, you said I was really good with Danny."

"Yes, I did," Pat admitted.

"And you'll be just as good with Andrea's new horse," Mr. Cummings said swiftly. "I just bought a beauty for her. A genuine champion. But this time she must be ready. It's ridiculous not to win. Janie, now come along. Danny's not going quite yet. Arrangements have to be made. It's hard to get rid of a lame pony." He looked helplessly at Pat. There was nothing he could say.

Back at home, Janie watched Mike closely as he and William practiced playing the harmonica. She had to admit Mike was patient. He was gentle. But Janie pulled herself up sharply. We don't need him around, she reminded herself.

"Hey, William," Mike's voice was playful. "You've got the most important thing it takes to be a great player.

Breath!" William caught the joke and laughed. Janie found herself smiling at William's look of doggy devotion.

"Janie, I want to talk to you." Mrs. Neely was on the couch marking papers, the first writing assignment she had given to her summer students. She put down her pencil and looked at Janie. Janie had a good idea what her mother was about to say. "Sit down here next to me. Now Janie, you had no right to talk to Mr. Cummings about keeping that pony. I've never asked any favors from anyone. You're my daughter, so you don't need any favors either."

Janie didn't answer, and her mother went on. "Mr. Cummings has been most generous to you. And if he thinks it's best to get rid of that horse, so be it."

51

"But it's not 'that horse'," cried Janie. "It's Danny!"

Mrs. Neely eased up a little when she saw Janie's beet-red face. "Janie, love, there's so much more in the world than horses and riding."

Janie couldn't say anything. Mrs. Neely shook her head. "All right then. Tomorrow I want you to go to Mr. Cummings and apologize for trying to interfere. Do you understand, Janie?"

Janie nodded. She stumbled toward the stairs and the comfort of her room. She knew Mike had heard it all. That made everything worse.

William peered into Janie's darkened room later that evening. Muffled sobs rose from the bed.

"Janie," he began. "Maybe the new horse will be a thousand times better than Danny. And you'll be riding it and training it. So what's the difference?"

"It wouldn't be the same. It wouldn't be Danny." William patted his sister gently, pushed his glasses more firmly on his nose and left quietly.

Ten

Apologizing to Mr. Cummings was not going to be easy. Janie dawdled gloomily across the meadows and finally found herself in the graceful Cummings' living room. Mr. Cummings did not notice her at first as she stood in the arched dining room entrance. He was once again engrossed in his newspaper, his morning coffee beside him. At last he looked up.

"Ah, Janie. Just the person I want to see." He didn't sound angry.

"Mr. Cummings—er—I have to apologize. I mean I shouldn't have tried to make you keep Danny. It's just that . . ."

But Mr. Cummings held up his hand, smiling. "No need to go on, my dear." He paused dramatically. "Janie, the thing you wanted most—you've got it. You have yourself a pony." There was a buzzing in Janie's ears. She knew she must have heard wrong. She tried to speak, but he was first.

"You don't understand? Well it's really very simple. A certain person, who does not wish to be known, has advanced the money. It wasn't much, not for a lame pony," he added comfortably.

"I don't understand. You mean Danny? Someone gave Danny to me?" Janie began to leap, dance and sing inside. But outside she remained still and controlled.

"But who . . .?" Janie asked.

"That must remain a secret. Now, this is the arrangement that was suggested. You will have two animals to take care of. Your own, and Andrea's new horse. You will earn Danny's feed that way. Of course, Andrea's Thoroughbred will need special attention and training for showing. But the pony—he's yours to do what you can with. How does that strike you?"

Janie's voice shook. "I—I think it's great. I'll work hard. I really will, Mr. Cummings." He nodded, anxious to get back to his reading. But as she edged out of the room he stopped her.

"Oh, Janie. Someone certainly has a lot of faith in you. You should be very pleased."

"I am, Mr. Cummings. I am." Carefully she walked

across the huge paneled room. Carefully she opened the terrace door and closed it behind her. Then the joy welled up and she seemed to fly all the way home. She rushed into the garden, over the porch, and burst into the cottage.

"Mom! Mom! Guess what! Danny's mine, Mom. Danny belongs to me. Now he won't have to go."

Kate Neely was setting out for her summer teaching job. She met Janie in the hall and looked at her excited daughter, amused at the complete transformation.

"Yes, it's marvelous, darling, Mr. Cummings called me earlier. I admit I was against it at first. We're not the horse-owning kind of people. But I know how you love that pony, and I know you'll keep your side of the bargain."

"Isn't Pat wonderful, Mom? She did this for me."

"How do you know who your mysterious benefactor is, Janie?" Mrs. Neely asked.

"I just know. After all, who else could it be?"

Danny seemed to know Janie was helping him. He stood still, only moving his tail to flick away flies, while Janie held the hose close. Janie let the cool water trickle down over the injured leg. From time to time, the pony snorted gently into her hair. William sat on a nearby log looking like a messy little owl. There was a puzzled expression on his face.

"Janie," he said finally, "how come Danny looks like a horse and yet you keep saying he's a pony?"

"It's because he's fourteen hands high. If he had been just a bit bigger, he'd be a small horse instead of a large pony."

"Hands?" William's voice rose in disbelief.

"Yes, hands. That's four inches. And you measure from here." She pointed to the base of Danny's neck on his back, right over his front leg.

William seemed satisfied. The two of them were silent for a while. Then William spoke up in his "I've caught you" voice.

"Janie, what if two horses got married and had a baby that didn't grow too tall? Like you, Janie. Would that be a pony or a horse?"

"William, horses do not get married. They mate. Pat says always use the right words for things."

"All right. Mate. What then?"

Janie tried to think of an answer. William should have gone to day camp. He was a little nuisance, always asking weird questions. "Well, I suppose they would have a pony," she decided.

"Yes, but Janie . . ." He began again. Then he stopped short.

Pat had come out of the stable. She bent over to zip up her worn and shiny chaps. Her hair was caught back in a bandana. "How's it going?" she asked Janie cheerfully.

"Great. And Pat, you don't have to worry. I'm going to work really hard to show my thanks."

"I'm sure you are. But Dr. Greaves is not at all convinced Danny will be any good to show again. You do realize that, don't you, Janie?"

"But there's a chance, isn't there?"

"Yes, there's a chance."

"And if he does get better, would it be wrong to jump him? Would his bad leg come back?"

"Janie, I guess it's like an athlete. You do as much as you can. And then you keep your fingers crossed." Pat noticed

56

William on his log. "Hello, William. How are you today?"

"Very well, thank you." He answered so politely that Janie turned around in amazement to look at him. She caught the look of pure devotion he directed toward Pat and smiled to herself.

The two of them watched as Pat made for the paddock. Janie sighed happily and said, "She got Danny for me, you know. She's just the most fantastic person that ever was." William nodded in agreement.

Janie was leading Danny carefully around the paddock, William trailing along behind her, when the big, blue horse van pulled into the stable yard. Andrea came running from the house. She stood to one side giving little squeals of delight, her hands fluttering to her throat. The doors were opened and the ramp let down. Andrea's new Thoroughbred had arrived.

Midnight Star was a strikingly handsome mare, finely built and gleaming ebony black. Her leg wrappings were snowy against her slender legs. She sniffed the air nervously. Danny lifted his ears and stared. The stable horses which had been grazing close by ambled to the fence one by one. Midnight Star flattened her ears, but Pat calmed her.

Andrea was ecstatic. "Oh, she's fabulous! Isn't she perfect, Pat? Let me take her up?"

"Be my guest." Pat handed the lead-line over and Andrea led the mare past the paddock. Janie smiled at the beautiful newcomer. Andrea just tossed her head and sniffed.

"Janie," she said spitefully, "I'm the only one who can ride Midnight Star. I don't want her going lame, too." And she shot a contemptuous glance at Danny. Janie bent her head, hurt. Later as she watched while Andrea gave Midnight Star her first workout, Janie turned to Danny and consoled him.

"Don't you worry, Danny. I'm going to get you all better." She promised herself she would not stop working until Danny could perform as well as Midnight Star.

Eleven

So began busy times for Janie. Early each morning she arrived at Longvue Farm stable. There were stalls to be mucked out and bedding to be changed. Bales of sweet-smelling hay needed stacking, only to disappear as hungry animals were fed. Sawdust was carted from the great tarpaulin-covered pile outside. Coats needed grooming, hooves were picked clean. Tails and manes grew knotty without constant care. Janie concentrated on Midnight Star and Danny. She grew fond of the sensitive black mare who responded so well to training. Janie did ride her, in spite of Andrea's declaration that *she* would be Midnight Star's only rider. It was Janie who was left with most of the exercising. And as Danny was carefully walked and his leg was hosed, his lameness lessened.

The day came when Mr. Cummings was called ringside to watch Andrea on Midnight Star. His daughter put the big horse through her paces. Midnight Star took the fences easily and responded to every lead. Mr. Cummings looked content and called out to Pat. "Well, what do you think? Will she be ready for the County Show on Labor Day?"

"If Andrea puts in some good hard work on her, I'd say yes."

Andrea rode over to her father and leaped down. She smiled up at him and fluttered her eyes as she had seen her mother do. "Oh, Daddy, isn't she just divine?" She

swung around to Janie, but now she was cool. "Here, walk her, Janie." Janie took the reins without a word.

Midnight Star was glad to get back to the shade of the stable. She shoved Janie gently out of the way, eager for her feed bucket. Danny was looking out of his stall. Janie fondled his head as she spoke to him. "It's all right Danny. I don't really care if you never jump again. I just want your leg to get better." She hugged him, pressing her cheek against his. She knew he understood.

Later that evening, Andrea decided to visit her horse. Over dinner she had told her parents her plans for her future, a future filled with prizes she would take on Midnight Star. In an overflow of generosity, she carried carrots, apples and greens to the stable. Pat had already checked the animals and closed up. Andrea turned on the stable lights and looked around. The horses blinked sleepily, straining to see who had come. The cats peered from their nests high on the hay bales. Andrea wobbled slightly in her high heels as she opened Midnight Star's stall.

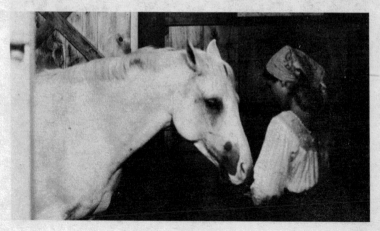

Soon there was grateful munching from Midnight Star and some jealous snorting from neighboring stalls. Andrea looked over at Danny. Impossible to think that she had never been able to conquer that stupid pony. Well, maybe an apple would work. She closed Midnight Star's stall and unlatched Danny's. The door slid aside noisily. Danny hovered uncertainly at the rear of the stall.

"Here, fellow." She held an apple at arm's length. He did not move. Impatiently, she stepped closer and thrust it upward toward his mouth. With a surprised whinny, he jerked his head and twisted away. Andrea was furious. She flung the apple down and marched out. She turned off the lights as she went. Gradually the stable settled down. Moonlight filtered into the stalls, and fell on the pale form of Danny as he sniffed curiously at his open door.

Twelve

Janie often wondered afterwards how she managed to get through that next day. She bounced into the stable before seven on that bright morning. As soon as she saw Pat's face she knew something had happened.

"Danny's gone."

It seemed impossible.

"Did you close his stall properly?" Pat asked.

Janie answered indignantly. "I always close it properly." That was true.

"I've called the town police. If he turns up they'll let us know." Pat reassured her. "There's no need to think the worst. He probably wandered off somewhere. He's sure to come back."

There was nothing to do but wait. The day dragged on. Janie finished her chores early. There was less to do without Danny. Andrea was strangely sympathetic. "Janie, I'm really sorry to hear about Danny," she said. But Janie could only smile weakly. She couldn't answer.

By late afternoon, there had been no word on Danny, and Janie decided to go home. Mr. Cummings sat on the ring rail as Midnight Star went through her training.

"If anyone sees the pony, we'll get a call right away," he told Janie soothingly.

"Thank you," she murmured.

"I know you've been doing a first class job, Janie," he said, trying to cheer her up. She looked across the ring to Andrea on Midnight Star. Then she turned to go.

Sadness settled over Janie. Instead of taking the short cut by the meadows, she decided to walk home along the road. Danny might have wandered along there. The shadows were lengthening. Only an occasional car or a distant dog's barking interrupted the woodland sounds. Janie strained to listen over the whirr of grasshoppers and the cries of birds. There was nothing. A squirrel broke cover and raced across the path ahead. Over and over Janie remembered how she had hugged Danny the evening before. Over and over she saw the empty stall.

"Danny," she called loudly. Then she tried again. "Danny." A path led into thick brush. It was hardly wide enough for a single car. Deeply rutted, strangely dark, it led into the woods. Janie paused uneasily. She knew better than to wander off into the woods alone. But surely this was different. She decided to follow the path, under the overhanging trees, past discarded garbage and broken television sets. Insects buzzed and clicked. It smelled damp and sour. What if Danny were lost in here? He would surely be afraid.

Was that the muffled whinny of a pony? An owl flew low overhead. Janie was nervous. Ahead she saw an old shack with a sagging porch. An ancient couch had been thrown into the bushes in front, and an empty drum and a battered tin tub stood surrounded by oily mud. Janie looked closer. Hoof prints! Someone was living here. Tinny music could be heard faintly. Janie approached with caution.

To one side a shed was almost covered by thick vine-like weeds. Its entrance was a dark, jagged hole. Now Janie could really smell horses. A hoof struck the ground. A bridle jangled. With a wary eye on the house, Janie moved toward the shed. She peered into the deep shadows.

"Danny?" Her voice trembled and shivered. "Danny?" Yes, there was an animal inside. It swung round, staring in her direction. Janie drooped in disappointment. An elderly brown draft horse regarded her calmly. Beside it were an anvil and other tools.

She heard a sudden sharp snapping of twigs. Janie edged fearfully into the dimness of the shed. She backed up toward the rear wall. Her elbow knocked over an empty can. It fell to the ground with a clatter.

"Who's there?" a harsh voice roared. "Who's back there?" A massive shape filled the doorway and advanced on Janie. There was nothing to do but make a run for it. Janie reached the door when a huge hand gripped her arm and dragged her, blinking and panting, out into the light. The face was unshaven. The eyes were angry.

"Going to steal from me, were you?" the man yelled at her.

"No! I wasn't stealing." She struggled, but his rough fingers dug in deeper. At last a woman's voice cut shrilly across the roar.

"Jethro, you leave her be. You hear me?" Sullenly, the man let go of Janie's arm. His dirt-streaked face was twisted.

Behind Jethro a frail woman stood defiantly. A plump baby rested on one hip. Clinging to her wrinkled skirt was a small thin girl as grubby as her mother. But Jethro's wife was not afraid.

65

"You can beat up on your own kids. But you'd better not do it to someone else's," she shouted.

Jethro muttered to himself angrily. The woman leaned forward to see Janie better.

"I declare. Ain't you Miz Neely's child?"

"Yes."

"Her ma is Sybil's tutor. And she don't have no pa." She turned on her enormous husband.

"Then why's she trying to steal from me," he whined.

"I wasn't trying to steal." Janie retorted. "I was looking for my pony. He's lost. He's been gone since last night."

Jethro backed off. He picked up a hammer from a peg outside the smithy. "Well, he sure ain't here. So git. I got work to do," he growled.

Janie rubbed her arm. It was aching now. The small girl watched her curiously, twisting one dirty scarred leg around the other. She gave a gap-toothed smile.

"You remember me to your ma. She's a real nice lady," the woman said as she shifted her baby on her hip. They stood in the same spot while Janie left.

If only it had been Danny in the shed. Janie would have done anything to rescue him. Anything.

She did not hear the noise at first. Then it came again. "Psst." She lifted her head nervously. It was the pale boy from the horse show. He stepped out from the shelter of a wrecked and rusted automobile. Unkempt as he was his smile was friendly and open.

"Oh, it's you." She stared at him warily.

"I live back there." He thrust his thumb toward the shack. "Name's Otis." He examined her silently. Then, "Pa lit into you, huh?"

"I was only looking for my pony."

"What happened to him?"

"He's lame. And he's been missing all day." The boy's face fell.

"I'll keep an eye out for him." He tried to sound grown up. Janie nodded silently.

"Hey!" He called out as she passed. "My dad. He's not as bad as he sounds. Are you going to be at the big County Show?"

"Maybe."

"I might see you there," he said.

67

The fields by the Neely cottage were golden in the late afternoon sun. When Mike drove up, Mrs. Neely and Janie were talking in the garden.

"Any news?" he asked.

"Nothing." Kate Neely shook her head. "Janie had her own bit of excitement." She described the incident in the woods. Mike looked seriously at Janie.

"I was sure Danny was there." Janie hastened to explain. "That man—his name's Jethro—you should see where they live. It's awful. So dirty and old."

"I know Jethro Harper." Mike said. "Works as a blacksmith, when he can. Plus any odd jobs he can find. Bit too much booze though, I'm afraid." He suddenly changed his expression. His eyes twinkled.

"Miss Janie," he declared with mock gallantry, "I am here to serve. Shall we go?"

Janie was puzzled. She glanced at her mother and back at Mike. "You came just because of Danny?"

"Well, I thought you could use a helping hand." Mike put a friendly arm around her shoulder and they walked out to the pickup truck. "We've got a little daylight left. I know the back roads around here. I thought we could scoot around and see what's what."

Janie beamed. She had recovered. "Could we?" Her voice was high with new hope. "He couldn't have gone far with his leg."

"Leave a candle in the window for us." Mike waved to Mrs. Neely.

Together they rode down the nearby roads and lanes. Mike stopped at farmhouses and stores, asking whether a gray pony had come that way. Only as darkness began to fall did Janie lose hope. She shivered and settled closer to Mike. She was tired and disheartened when they reached the Neely home.

"We'll try again tomorrow. I promise you."

"Thank you, Mr. De . . ." Janie caught herself. "Thank you, Mike."

She lingered outside, scanning the hedges and fields, trying to see through the deepening darkness.

"Danny," she called softly, not really expecting him to hear.

By daybreak, Janie felt as though she had been miserable all her life. She got out of bed and looked at herself solemnly in her mirror. Her eyes were swollen. Her hair was matted and damp. Her nose was red. She found her clothes and went off for a long shower.

Later, Janie sat wearily on the porch. She could think only of Danny. She got up and wandered aimlessly around the cottage, kicking at tufts of grass, clenching her teeth fiercely as she remembered the first time she had seen him. The air was crisp. Fall would soon be here. Was it a noise that warned her? Or just a feeling? Janie looked up and frowned. Quietly, she turned the corner of the cottage. And there she stopped, stock-still.

Facing her, gazing straight at her, was Danny! Surely, Janie decided, it's a dream. He was bedraggled and scratched up, but it was Danny, all right. He tossed his head in greeting.

"Danny," she murmured. Her voice broke. "Oh, Danny." The big pony ambled toward her. His head was hugged, his neck stroked, his nose kissed. When Janie stopped he prodded her for more until she was laughing through her tears.

"Mom!" she finally called. "Mom! It's Danny. I was searching for him. But he came and found me. He's never even been here before." She called again. "And Mom. He's not limping anymore. Come and see!" It was true. The limp had gone.

Thirteen

A jubilant Janie listened to Dr. Greaves.

"The cuts are superficial, of course. Probably got them rubbing against some barbed wire. Most important, the leg looks as if it really has improved. For the moment."

"He's had some pretty good care, wouldn't you say?" Pat asked the veterinarian.

"I certainly would. But lameness is always a tricky business. So you're the new owner, Janie? Well, you've looked after this pony very well. And now you've got yourself a great little animal." Janie nodded and gave

Danny a brisk slap on the back to hide her pleasure. Maybe I'll be a veterinarian like Dr. Greaves when I grow up, she thought.

"Why don't you put Danny in his stall, Janie. He's had a tough time," Pat suggested.

When they were alone, Pat questioned Dr. Greaves.

"The leg could go again, couldn't it?"

He shrugged. "There may be a basic weakness. An old injury that never healed."

"And meanwhile?"

"Pat." He was impatient now. "You know the answer. You're a pro. The girl has her pony. Let her really enjoy him."

Enjoy Danny Janie did. She worked him carefully but firmly. Within days he was back to his old form. Janie picked up every pointer she could from Pat. When Andrea took lessons on Midnight Star, Janie would follow behind on Danny. Equitation became Janie's passionate interest. She hardly noticed the differences between herself and Andrea. Janie's faded jeans and her comfortable shirts

were natural to her. Andrea's riding outfits varied with her moods. And Andrea had a natural elegance which sat well on the glossy black horse. But Danny was groomed as perfectly as any horse in the stable.

It was later that week when Mike De Vito strolled across the stable yard and propped himself against a tree.

"Shorten your reins, Andrea. Let's have sharper responses." Pat called from the ring center. "Come on now. Liven up. What if you were at the County Show this minute?"

Behind Andrea, Janie sat on Danny, listening intently. She too checked her reins and straightened her back. Her face too had the aloof calm of the competitor. Mike smiled to himself. At first he watched unobserved. Finally, Pat strode over.

"Well, and what has the lonesome prairie sent us?" she teased.

"Just visiting the civilized folks." He drawled in his best Western manner. They laughed comfortably. Mike became serious. "I wanted to see the pony that's been causing all this commotion," he confessed. "Hey, Janie's really good, isn't she?"

"She most certainly is."

"You mean that?"

"Didn't you know, cowboy? I always mean what I say. She could be a little star."

Andrea swung Midnight Star to a stop in front of them.

"Pat, is this my lesson? Or isn't it?" Her voice was sharp. But she flashed a smile to Mike.

"Yes, Andrea. This is your lesson," Pat answered with mock weariness. "Come again, cowboy," she said as she walked away.

Janie led a tired Danny out of the ring.

"What are you doing here?" she asked brightly. She was glad to see Mike.

"Just driving by. So that's the famous Danny?" He stroked the pony casually.

"Isn't he great? He's still a bit stiff when he moves. But Dr. Greaves says he'll probably get better." Her face shone with affection.

"He's a fine-looking fellow," Mike agreed. "When you're through, I'll give you a ride home."

So Mike would be spending the evening with them again. Some of the old wariness came back.

"I have to cool Danny out first," she mumbled.

"My life story. Waiting for the ladies." And Mike opened the gate with such a flourish that Janie giggled in spite of

74

herself. Mike watched Andrea's final exercises while he waited. His face had grown thoughtful.

Janie was silent on the drive home. It had been a busy day. Besides, sitting next to Mike reminded her of the search for Danny. Mike had been great then, she found herself thinking. Just like a real . . . .

"Where are your thoughts, Janie?" he asked.

She hesitated. "Did you know my father?"

"No. And I'm sorry I never did. Your mother says he was a wonderful man."

"I don't really remember him much," Janie admitted. "But he was a good rider. He had his own horse too, you know."

"Yes. So I hear."

Suddenly Janie felt more relaxed. As though the air had been cleared. They said nothing more for the rest of the brief drive. But it was an easy silence. There were a million questions Janie wanted to ask Mike. Had he ever been married? Did he ever have any children? But somehow she knew they could wait.

Mrs. Neely was unloading groceries at the cottage.

"What a nice surprise." Her welcome included them both. "How did you two meet up?"

"I had a meeting with some clients. But I was early, so I decided to do a little taxi work and bring home the working girl. Janie, here, she's the one with the surprises. Did you ever see her ride?" Janie felt her face flush at the compliment.

Mrs. Neely's expression revealed nothing. "Is she really good?" she asked lightly.

"I think she's all right." His tone said more than that. "In fact, I had an idea. And I like it. Why can't Janie here enter the next horse show on Danny?"

"Well, I don't know," said Mrs. Neely. "Could Danny do it?"

"His leg seems all better." Janie's voice rose with the excitement in her. Oh, please, please, she begged silently.

"Mom?"

Kate Neely's face was thoughtful.

"Janie," she began. "Are you sure you're not trying to be someone you're not?" She spoke huskily. "I hate to think of you envying Andrea Cummings."

"Andrea? I never want to be like Andrea. I'm going to be like Pat."

Mrs. Neely gazed at her daughter. Suddenly she laughed. "I've got news for you, Janie. Remember, mothers *can* be wrong." Janie squinted in puzzlement.

"I mean you win, Janie. Both of you."

"I can show Danny?" Janie yelped.

"That's what I mean."

During the next day's practice, Danny made several good rounds. His jumping was mostly smooth and sure. He was taking leads smartly. Janie pulled him up beside Pat and looked down. Danny flipped his tail and snorted. Pat spoke.

"Janie, you asked me a question this morning. And now I have the answer. Yes, you are ready to show. And I think Danny is, too." Janie grinned, leaned over and plopped a kiss between Danny's two pointed ears. He simply shook his head, impatient to be back at work.

Fourteen

In the next two weeks Janie worked harder than she had ever thought possible. William complained loudly. Why did he have to give away six of his ten mice when Janie could smell up the whole place with horses? Janie just laughed at him, saying that horses smelled better than all the fancy perfumes in the world. Certainly better than a cage full of dirty mice.

There were evenings when she could scarcely drag herself home. But she never admitted that the work was too much. Her muscles were strong now. She had even grown. Her mother begged her to take time to go shopping. Her favorite old shirts were getting tight all of a sudden. But Janie preferred the stable, the ring, the trails. She took a packed lunch and often ate it alone, sitting under a tree, or on a hay bale in the stable. Here she could relax, lying back, the hay prickly against her skin, watching the birds which nested in the rafters. This was her world.

On just such a day, Andrea appeared in the doorway.

"Janie, saddle up Midnight Star and bring her to the ring. I'm taking her out on the trails this afternoon." Janie rose immediately and led the black mare to the crossties. Andrea paced impatiently outside the stable, slapping her crop against her field boots. Pat was there.

"Since when don't you saddle up your own horse, Andrea?" she asked sternly.

"She's supposed to work here, isn't she? So let her do her job." Andrea turned on her heel and entered the cool stable again.

She watched Janie moodily for a while. Then she spoke. "You're not really going to ride that Danny in the County Show, are you, Janie?" She sounded anxious.

"I'm going to enter one or two classes," Janie answered cautiously.

"You'd better make sure they're nice easy classes. Don't go trying for the Children's Hunter. He'd never make it." Janie finished saddling up the mare. "He's a lemon," Andrea went on. "That's what my father calls him. You know what your Danny will do, don't you? The same as he did with me. All those people, they'll scare him. And he'll shy. Or maybe he'll pull his fake lame act for you."

"It was not fake," Janie flared. Then she controlled herself. She passed the reins to Andrea.

"Just remember what I said. It'll be better for you," Andrea repeated as she led Midnight Star away. Janie turned to Danny and stroked him gently.

"Come on, Danny boy. Let's go and get some work done. No time for riding along the trails. We've got more important things to do."

Over dinner Andrea chattered about Midnight Star to her parents. But Mr. Cummings wasn't listening. The stock market was doing poorly. It was annoying. Mrs. Cummings meanwhile was concerned with her fall wardrobe. Her designer had left her a pile of darling sketches. If only Mr. Cummings would take time to look at them with her. Andrea was restless and bored. She wondered if she would ever do well enough with her riding to please her father. She took some carrots and a handful of sugar lumps and crossed the dark garden.

Around the stable all was quiet. The shifting of hooves and muffled snorts were the only sounds from the animals. Andrea opened the main door and switched on the light. A cat leaped out from near her foot. From its mouth hung the long limp tail of a mouse. Andrea jumped.

Midnight Star came quickly to the front of her stall. The other horses watched lazily. They expected no special treats. The mare munched noisily. Once again, it was Danny who drew Andrea's attention. The pale and luminous face glowed from the shadows. She stared at him hesitantly. She slid open his door and offered a sugar lump.

"You planning to leave the door open again, Andrea, like you did before?" Andrea was so startled she jumped. She twisted around and saw Pat standing in the shadows.

"I didn't mean to let him out," she protested. "It was an accident. Why would I do a thing like that? Pat, you won't tell my father, will you?"

Pat looked at her, suddenly sorry for the red-faced girl. "I haven't a clue why you'd do it. But I'll tell you what I know. From now on you are putting on and taking off your own saddle. Is that clear?" Pat asked in a stern voice. Andrea nodded hastily. "And you'll stop being a brat when it comes to Janie."

"I don't see why . . ." Andrea began. But one look at Pat's face silenced her. She nodded again. "All right."

Fifteen

The air was crisp when Janie rose at four on show day, and by the time they set out, Midnight Star and Danny looked impeccable in the bright September sunshine. A riding outfit lay across the back seat. Janie sneaked a look over her shoulder. Her jacket was dark brown. Inside the matching brown helmet were her gloves and the silver pin from Pat, in the image of a pony's head. For luck. Janie looked at her friend. Pat seemed tense today. Perhaps she was tired. Janie had never thanked her properly, and decided this would be the right moment.

"Pat, I owe all of this to you. Giving me Danny was the most wonderful thing anyone's ever done."

"Giving you Danny . . ." Pat began. "But Janie, much as I wanted you to have him, *I'm* not the one who gave him to you."

"But Pat . . . who was it, then?" Janie asked.

"I don't know. But you're right, it was a truly wonderful thing to do."

Janie settled back to watch the slowly awakening countryside as they drove along, surprised and puzzled to learn that she didn't know, after all, who had given Danny to her.

This time the show grounds were huge. Stately brick buildings and fine old gardens were everywhere. Low stables held resident horses. Temporary stalls had been erected for visitors. And they had come from near and far. Lines of vans and trailers filled the nearby pastures. Rings and courses had been roped or fenced for the events ahead. Striped awnings shielded the announcers and the tables filled with ribbons, cups and trophies. Already horses and ponies were in schooling rings. Some riders were already dressed to begin.

Once more Janie was entranced at the sight of so many animals. There was a sense of urgency, of constant activity. Many horses were nervous. But Danny enjoyed it all. He craned his neck to watch a Pinto pony cantering in a paddock. He whinnied in a friendly greeting to the bay Arab with the white blaze who peered out of an adjacent trailer. Janie knew her pony was in top form.

Janie worked her hands into the new gloves. She wriggled her fingers to ease the leather. Her hat sat well. She looked down at herself. Everything was in place.

"Wow! You look great." It was Otis Harper. He stared at her admiringly.

"How did you get here?" She looked behind him warily.

"Don't worry. My daddy ain't here. I hitched a ride." He grinned. "Pa's got a new job now. That feller who's here with your Mom. That's his boss."

"Mike?" Janie was bewildered.

"Is that his name? Mr. De Vito, I call him. He's great. He came to the house, saw my pa sitting there. And gave him a job. Just like that! He helps build houses now."

The loudspeaker crackled and an announcement was made.

Janie listened. "I have to go now. My class is next," she said.

"I'll give you a leg up," the boy said eagerly. He was stronger than he looked. When she was in her saddle he smiled up at her. "Some day, I'm going to be a show rider. Just like you."

It felt odd to have someone looking at her as if she were really special. Janie blushed. With a quick wave, the boy slipped behind the van and was gone.

"Have you seen? Little Janie's got herself a boyfriend." Janie did not look toward Andrea and her sniggering friend, Betty. And when Otis reappeared to tell her, "You're going to do great today. I'll be watching," Janie grinned at him for everyone to see.

The first equitation event was hard. Janie was self-conscious. As she circled Danny among the other entries in the ring, she could see her mother with Mike and William. Mr. and Mrs. Cummings were there too.

"Good luck, Janie darling," Mrs. Cummings called as she passed. Mrs. Neely beamed with pleasure to see the horses and ponies walking almost silently, their riders stern with concentration. The judge took careful notes. Pat watched her two charges closely. Janie and Andrea had started out fairly well. Pat frowned. She stood up straighter to see. No, it was no mistake! Andrea was deliberately letting Midnight Star block Danny, forcing him against the rail. The judge could not see what was happening! It was done so skillfully. Janie's face was as flushed and furious as Pat's. Mr. Cummings appeared to be unaware that anything was wrong.

The riders edged their mounts to the line-up to wait for the judge's final decision. "First . . . to Lucy Barnes of Plymouth Farm . . . on Cry Baby."

Andrea looked glum. "Second . . . to Andrea Cummings of Longvue Farm . . . on Midnight Star." Andrea prodded her mare to the ringmaster's side. She looked proudly toward her father. But Mr. Cummings shook his head slightly. Second was not good enough.

Pat pushed her way to the ring gate. The six winners filed out first. Then came Janie on Danny. She jumped down and stormed over to Andrea. "You did that on purpose. You worked me against the fence, just to get at Danny." Janie's helmet had slipped sideways. Her face was scarlet.

Andrea was amused. "Midnight Star doesn't need to do that to beat your stupid Danny."

"Andrea, get down." Pat's voice was icy. "I think I shall have to speak to your father. And I don't think he is going to like what I have to say."

83

"No, don't do that."

"Janie has two more classes. Is it agreed that you are to stay away from her?"

"All right." Andrea was sullen now.

"Andrea." Mr. Cummings had arrived. "Follow me. I want to talk to you." Pat and Janie exchanged looks.

"Poor Andrea." Pat shook her head. "Mr. Cummings does like being first. I saw what happened. It wasn't your fault. You ride well." Janie felt better. As long as Pat knew she had not let Danny down.

There was only enough time to cool Danny out and wipe him off before the next class. Janie was too rushed to be nervous. It was a second equitation class. The ringmaster gave his instructions and the group of riders circled their mounts: walk, trot, canter, turn. All went smoothly until the second canter, when a small child threw an ice-cream wrapper into the ring. It fell in Danny's path. With a jittery start, the pony reared and skipped sideways. A groan rose from the onlookers. Janie lost control for a few precious moments. Then Danny picked up his stride. But they were out of the running.

Janie's head was high at the final line-up.

"First prize . . . Andrea Cummings from Longvue Farm . . . on Midnight Star." Janie watched as the elegant black mare was ridden to the ringmaster. Midnight Star stood quietly while the blue ribbon was pinned to her bridle. Janie's mother smiled her encouragement. Janie leaned over and patted Danny.

It was getting cooler that afternoon when Janie gave her boots a last polish and brushed her jacket. Danny was sparkling clean again. He had rested. Now he was ready.

Janie touched up the ties on his mane. A large hand reached out and patted the pony.

"You looked very good in the last class. Both of you."

It was Mike. Janie was glad to see him. She was proud that he had come over to find her among the rows of trailers.

"I should have noticed the ice-cream wrapper," she said.

"These things can happen to anyone. From where I sat I thought you handled it like a real pro."

Janie touched Danny's soft nose gently. She looked up at Mike, suddenly angry. "It's just not fair."

"But you rode him in the show. That's what counts."

"It's not that. Mr. Cummings says Danny's just a lemon."

"That's one opinion. We don't happen to agree, do we?"

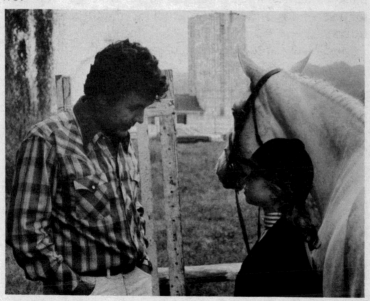

Janie shook her head. Her throat tightened. She smiled at Mike. "You never did agree, did you? It was you, all along. You lent the money so I could get Danny. And I was sure all the time it was Pat."

"My big secret! Who told you?"

"No one had to tell me. But I should have guessed right away. You believed in Danny when nobody else did. Just like you believe in Mr. Harper." She sounded triumphant. She had found him out.

A weary group of horse lovers gathered for one of the show's main events, the Children's Hunter. But the riders and their mounts could show no signs of fatigue. One at a time they must take to the huge course. Walls and fences were to be jumped in the order memorized from the ringmaster's instructions. Later, the circuit would be repeated for a second round. It was a grueling trial for animals and riders.

Mrs. Neely and Mike waited eagerly with William. Mr.

and Mrs. Cummings had settled themselves in lawn chairs on the far side of the smooth green enclosure. Pat remained with the competitors answering questions, giving last minute advice. The riders concealed their nervousness. They seemed detached and calm, like their mounts, as they waited their turns.

Andrea was called first. Midnight Star trotted out, dark coat gleaming, her tail held high. She settled into her pace. Janie could see her take the first fences. A murmur of approval was heard from the crowd. By the time they returned, Andrea's face was flushed and her horse was streaked with sweat. Janie's hands grew moist under her gloves. Otis popped up beside her, hands clasped champion-style over his head. He gave her a perky salute. Janie tried hard to concentrate, to learn from watching. When her own name crackled over the loudspeaker, she took a deep breath and rode Danny out into the field. The pony cantered nicely. His mane and tail picked up the gold of the low sun. He relished the empty course ahead of him. Janie felt him flying under her. When he clipped a bar her heart dropped. But the bar did not fall and they soon finished the circuit. How had they done? Only the judge, high at his post in the middle of the course, could see every fence, count every fault.

Andrea's second round was applauded. Midnight Star pranced out imperiously and gave a flashy performance. With her slender rider she made a graceful picture. The strain showed when they left the ring. Sweat coursed down the black mare's sides now. Andrea held herself erect and ignored the aches in her body. Janie smiled at her in friendship and Andrea, a little uncertainly, smiled back.

It was with a lighter heart that Janie took her second

round. "All right, Danny. Now. The best we can." And Danny let himself go. Janie only knew that it felt good. The crowds flashed past in a blur. She heard the pony grunt with effort. She felt his sweat on her legs. Trees, bushes, people, fences, all dissolved into one and then it was over. A burst of applause, a whoop or two, and Janie could relax.

Slowly she dismounted and stroked the weary pony. They watched the last riders. There were some mishaps. Even a tumble, which left Janie gasping in sympathy. But the far fences were out of sight. She couldn't guess at what was happening there. One thing she was sure of: Danny had competed. He had finished the course. She looked at him affectionately. He nudged her in his old way, knocking her hat to one side, leaving a smear of saliva in her hair.

She pushed him off, laughing. There was a commotion. Announcements were made. Pat was next to her, shaking her shoulder.

"Janie, what's the matter? Didn't you hear?" It came again, more clearly this time.

"The Blue Ribbon . . . and the trophy . . . go to the winner, from Longvue Farm, Janie Neely . . . on Danny."

A dazed Janie straightened her helmet. Andrea stepped close. "You did well, Janie. Congratulations!" She said it quietly, almost like the Andrea of last summer. Janie gave Danny one kiss and led him out.

"Second . . . from Longvue Farm . . . Andrea Cummings on Midnight Star."

Janie headed the line of winners as they jogged out to the center of the course where the judge awaited them. The horses and ponies trotted behind their riders, heads bobbing. It was a long and joyous run. Janie saw the smiling faces of the judge and of the ringmaster who

pinned on Danny's blue ribbon and handed her the large silver plate. Then she led the group back to the gate.

They passed Mr. and Mrs. Cummings. "Incredible," he muttered, "Quite incredible." But Mrs. Cummings clapped for all the performers, charmed at the picture they presented, happy for Janie as much as for her daughter. At last Janie reached Pat at the staging area.

"You see, Janie. What did I tell you? All it takes is a lot of hard work. And maybe a little love!" Pat ran her hand expertly over Danny's shoulder as she spoke. By now Mike had arrived. Janie's mother and William were not far behind. Janie looked up at the big man who had helped make her dreams come true.

"Well, Janie, it all happened the way you planned. Now what?"

At first Janie was unable to answer. She paused and then was matter-of-fact.

"First of all, I have to cool Danny out." She led her pony toward the vans where he could be rested. The small group stood watching each with his or her own thoughts. Mrs. Neely made to follow Janie, but Pat put out a hand and prevented her.

"Don't go," she said. "Look at Danny." They looked, and Mrs. Neely gasped. The pony's limp had returned.

"He did it for Janie," Mike whispered. "What a champion!"

Much later a weary Janie, alone with her Danny at last, held her cheek next to his. She gazed up at him lovingly through her tears and whispered, as much to herself as to him, "Don't worry, Danny. I got you better once and I'll get you better again. I'll be with you all the time. Anyway we did it. We showed them you're special. We showed them you're a champion!"

BACKGROUND NOTES

"DANNY" is based on a true story. Rebecca Page, the eighth-grader who plays Janie, really nursed a lame pony named Danny back to health. Rebecca had worked on a one-minute commercial and a short film called "Ronnie's Tune" with director Gene Feldman. Gene was so touched by Rebecca's dedication to her pony that he decided to make a movie out of her experience. Rebecca's story became the film, "DANNY."

Rebecca did not ride her own pony in the film. Instead, a horse named William Tell "acted" the role of Danny. Barbara Jean Ehrhardt, the accomplished horsewoman who plays Andrea in the film, rode her own horse.

"DANNY" was filmed on location in New York State, Connecticut and New Jersey, on estates and at local horse shows. Shooting took forty-three days, most of which were the hottest days of the summer months. Conditions were difficult for the crew, the actors and the horses. Rebecca's hard work and dedication on the set so impressed Gene that when filming was complete, he gave her William Tell as a special bonus.

IF YOU LIKED THIS BOOK,
YOU'LL LOVE THE FILM VERSION OF DANNY

TANNER-NATIONAL INC.
PRESENTS
A GENE FELDMAN FILM

STARRING

REBECCA PAGE as *Janie Neely* and WILLIAM TELL as *Danny*

CAST

JANET ZARISH as *Pat Chapin*
BARBARA JEAN EHRHARDT as *Andrea Cummings*
GLORIA MADDOX as *Mrs. Kate Neely*
GEORGE LUCE as *Mr. Mike De Vito*
MICHAEL COERVER as *Mr. Monty Cummings*
ZACHARY DANZIGER as *William Neely*
JO ANNE PALMER as *Mrs. Vicky Cummings*
DR. WILLIAM BRADLEY as *Dr. Greaves*
RUTH ANN BOWERS as *Betty*
GEORGE CLARK HOSMER as *Jethro*
MICHAEL DANA as *Otis*

PRODUCTION

Produced and Directed by GENE FELDMAN
Executive Producer, JERRY FELDMAN
Original Screenplay by GENE FELDMAN & SUZETTE WINTER
A WOMBAT PRODUCTION

Associate Producer . . . . SUZETTE WINTER
Film Editor . . . . GLORIA WHITTEMORE
Music . . . . HARRY MANFREDINI
Director of Photography . . . . OLIVER WOOD
Production Manager . . . . BILL TASGAL
First Assistant Director . . . . RICHARD CAMP
Assistant Camera . . . . RICHARD DISTEFANO
Sound . . . . ROLF PARDULA
Air Director . . . . AUDREY RUBIN
Makeup . . . . JOAN PUMA
JANE FORTH
Script Supervisor . . . . TILLIE MARTIN
Wardrobe . . . . KAREN GALINAUGH
Hair Stylist . . . . VINCENT LOBRUTTO
Still Photographer . . . . CARL ROMANO
Casting . . . . BILL WILLIAMS

MPAA Rating: Ⓖ
(General Audiences—All Ages Admitted.)
Running Time: 90 minutes
World Premiere: June 23, 1979; Orpheum Theater; Memphis,
Tennessee

THE CRITICS LOVE DANNY!

" 'Danny' has irresistible appeal to everyone who enjoys stories about kids and horses."

—*Scholastic Magazine*
Margaret Ronan

"All young horse people will see themselves in this film. A touching film that young horse lovers no matter what their experience will treasure."

—*Horse Show Magazine*
Gerald A. Caserto, Jr.

"A sweet tale. . . .[with] talented newcomers, handsome horses."

—*Seventeen Magazine*
Edwin Miller

"A beautifully photographed story . . . an excellent film . . . and a treat for people who love horses."

—*National Board of Review*
Robert Martin

ABOUT THE AUTHOR

SUZETTE WINTER was born in England and has lived in France, Hong Kong, and Australia. Now an American citizen, she has worked as a film writer and as a script supervisor. In the course of her film assignments, she has worked on location in Mexico, the Soviet Union, Puerto Rico, and throughout the United States.

Suzette met Gene Feldman, who is her husband, while he was filming in Australia. In addition to working together on the production of "DANNY," Suzette was co-producer with Gene on the documentary films "HOLLYWOOD'S CHILDREN" and "THE HORROR OF IT ALL," both telecast on the PBS network.

 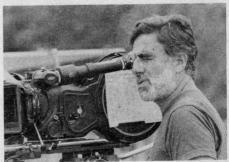

ABOUT THE PRODUCER/DIRECTOR OF THE MOVIE

GENE FELDMAN has been an English teacher, a book editor, and a playwright and has been involved in virtually every aspect of film making. He was a writer/producer on the NBC-TV series, "NEW YORK ILLUSTRATED," and was a writer/director on the ABC-TV series for kids, "DISCOVERY." His educational films have won him many awards.

In 1970, Gene and Suzette founded Wombat Productions, and since that time their films have been seen in classrooms in every state. "DANNY" is Wombat's first feature film. Most recently, Gene was writer and director of the documentary films "HOLLYWOOD'S CHILDREN" and "THE HORROR OF IT ALL."

This edition copyright © by Wieser & Wieser, Inc.
and Richard Horner Associates, 1990.

This edition published in 1990 by Gallery Books,
an imprint of W. H. Smith Publishers, Inc.,
112 Madison Avenue, New York, NY 10016.

Gallery Books are available for bulk purchase for sales
promotions and premium use. For details write or telephone
Manager of Special Sales, W. H. Smith Publishers, Inc.,
112 Madison Avenue, New York, NY 10016. (212) 532-6600

Illustrations copyright © by Berta and Elmer Hader, 1928.

ISBN 0-8317-42712

Printed in Hong Kong

THE LITTLE RED HEN

ILLUSTRATED BY BERTA † ELMER HADER

GALLERY BOOKS

ONCE upon a time there was a Little Red Hen.

She lived in a little white house with a Frog and a Cat.

The Cat wouldn't do any work. The Frog wouldn't do any work either. The Little Red Hen had to do the work all by herself.

This is what happened one morning in the little white house.

The Little Red Hen said, "It's breakfast time. Who is going to build the fire?"

The Frog said, "I won't."

The Cat said, "I won't."

The Little Red Hen said, "I will."

So she built a fine hot fire in the stove.

"Who is going to bake a cake for breakfast?" asked the Little Red Hen.

The Frog said, "I won't."

The Cat said, "I won't."

The Little Red Hen said, "I will."

So she mixed the cake and put it in the oven to bake.

When the cake was in the oven, the Little Red Hen said, "Who is going to set the table for breakfast?"

The Frog said, "I won't."

The Cat said, "I won't."

The Little Red Hen said, "I will."
So she put all the dishes on the table.

The Little Red Hen looked in the oven and saw that the cake was finished. She took it out and put it on a plate and carried it toward the table.

The Cat had her napkin unfolded and was all ready to eat the cake.

The Frog had his knife in one hand and his fork in the other. He was all ready to eat the cake.

The Little Red Hen stood still and looked at them.

She said, "Who will eat the cake?"

The

Frog

said,

"I will."

The

Cat

said,

"I will."

But the Little Red Hen said, "No, you won't!" And with the cake under her wing she flew right out the door.

On and on flew the Little Red Hen. At last she came to a hill where the sun was warm.

"Now," said the Little Red Hen, "I can eat all the cake myself."

On the other side of the hill lived the Fox family.

Father Fox woke up and yawned and stretched. He was very hungry.

The three little Foxes woke up. They cried and sulked. They were very hungry, too.

Mother Fox looked in the cupboard. There was nothing there for her family to eat for breakfast.

Father Fox picked up his big bag and went out to find them some food.

Over the hill he went, along the road.

Finally he came to a nice green, sunny field on the other side of the hill. There he stood still.

"That smell is nice. It must be fresh cake," he said.

He sniffed again.

"I smell a Little Red Hen, too," he said.

And sure enough, there was the Little Red Hen eating the cake.

The Fox walked quietly up behind her and popped her into his bag.

Then off he started toward home.

The Little Red Hen was very frightened.

She put her hand into her pocket to find her handkerchief and there she found her scissors.

Very carefully she cut a hole in the bag and stuck out her head. The Fox was just starting up a high hill, covered with big stones.

The Fox climbed the hill very slowly and the Little Red Hen had time to cut a big hole in the bag.

While the Fox was resting a minute she hopped out of the bag and found a big stone. She took the stone and put it into the bag.

When the Fox went on up the hill he thought, "How very heavy the Little Red Hen is."

Mother Fox
and one of the
little Foxes were
waiting for him at
the door.

"The kettle is
on the fire and the
water is boiling,"
she said when she
saw he had some-
thing for breakfast.

She took off the lid and the steam came out in clouds.

The three little Foxes played on the floor.

They were happy because they were going to have some breakfast.

Father Fox took his bag off his shoulders and opened it. He turned it upside down and emptied it into the pot.

There was a great splash!

Some of the water, which was very hot, hit Father Fox but he was not badly burned because he jumped back quickly.

Father Fox went to the kettle and peeped in.

Mother Fox went to the kettle and peeped in.

The three little Foxes went to the kettle and peeped in.

And then they all laughed.

"The Little Red Hen was very clever," said Father Fox, "I'm glad she's safe."

Then he went out into the garden and picked some beets for breakfast.

The Little Red Hen waited till the Fox had disappeared and then she flew home. She flew very fast but it was dark before she saw her little white house.

When she reached the garden she heard someone say, "I wish the Little Red Hen were here."

It sounded like the Frog's voice.

Then she heard someone else say, "I wish the Little Red Hen were here."

It sounded like the Cat's voice.

"Here I am," said the Little Red Hen.

The Frog started to scrub the floor.

"I'll never be lazy again," he said.

The Cat began to wash the clothes.

"I'll never be lazy again," she said.

And the Frog never was lazy again.

And the Cat never was lazy again.

And the Little Red Hen never had been lazy at all so they all worked together in the little white house and were happy all the day long.

FINIS